CARMEN

CARMEN

An Urban Adaptation of the Opera by

WALTER DEAN MYERS

EGMONT
USA
NEW YORK

ACKNOWLEDGMENTS

The author would like to thank Kwame Brandt-Pierce for his modern take on
Georges Bizet's music; Daniel Burwasser, PhD, of New York City's Talent Unlimited
High School for the Performing Arts, for his advice on the scores; and Julio and
Rob Guzman and Nico Medina for their help on the Spanish text.

EGMONT

We bring stories to life

First published by Egmont USA, 2011
443 Park Avenue South, Suite 806
New York, NY 10016

Copyright © Walter Dean Myers, 2011
Based on the opera *Carmen*; composer: Georges Bizet;
librettists: Henri Meilhac and Ludovic Halévy
All rights reserved

1 3 5 7 9 8 6 4 2

www.egmontusa.com
www.walterdeanmyers.net

Library of Congress Cataloging-in-Publication Data
Myers, Walter Dean
Carmen : an urban adaptation / by Walter Dean Myers.
p.   cm.
Summary: A policeman's obsessive love for a tempestuous wig factory worker ends in tragedy in
this updated version of Bizet's *Carmen*, set in Spanish Harlem, and told in screenplay format.
ISBN 978-1-60684-115-0 (hardcover) —
ISBN 978-1-60684-199-0 (electronic book) — ISBN 978-1-60684-192-1 (lib. bdg.)
[1. Love—Fiction. 2. Hispanic Americans—Fiction. 3. New York (N.Y.)—Fiction.]
I. Bizet, Georges, 1838–1875. Carmen. II. Title.
PZ7.M992Car 2011
[Fic]—dc22   2011002491

Printed in the United States of America

CPSIA tracking label information:
Random House Production • 1745 Broadway • New York, NY 10019

Contents

*A musical symbol 𝄞 within the text points out which songs can be found in the back of the book.

Cast of Characters

Carmen, 18, *Factory Worker*
José, 21, *Police Officer*
Escamillo, 28, *Rapper Turned Filmmaker*
Micaela, 20, *Teacher's Aide*
Zuniga, 36, *Police Sergeant*
Frasquita, 18, *Carmen's Best Friend*
Mercedes, 17, *Carmen's Friend*
Dancairo, 34, *Racketeer*
Raimondo, 37, *Racketeer*

Neighborhood Residents
Geraldo, 43, *Restaurant Owner*

Elena, 27

Maria, 22

Angel, 17

Juan, 55

Jimenez, 53

Carlos, 18

Tía Sofia, 67

Gato, 18

Manny, 18

Officer Shea, 23, *Police Officer*
Officer Lane, 24, *Policer Officer*
Gordito, 19, *Escamillo's Assistant*
Teresa, 40, *Fortune-teller*
Rami, 17, *Computer Wizard*
Yoshiro, 17, *Computer Wizard*

Act One

Scene 1

It is summer of the present time in Spanish Harlem. We hear the opening music as people go about their daily lives. To stage right, flags from the Dominican Republic, Puerto Rico, Cuba, and Mexico fly from a lamppost near a bench in a small square.

At center stage, stairs lead to a well-worn factory building bearing a sign reading DELGADO'S WIGS. Next to the factory, stage left, is a walk-up apartment house. Next to that is a restaurant, Gallina's.

A brown-skinned woman is sitting in one of the apartment-house windows. Two men are playing dominoes on an overturned box, a street vendor is selling multicolored ices, and several young men are simply standing around, almost as if they are part of the scenery, when they aren't eyeing some pretty women in short skirts and tight pants.

GERALDO, the owner of Gallina's, steps outside. Two neighborhood women, ELENA and MARIA, have been chatting out front.

GERALDO
Hey, chicas, I'm looking for a young man to help out around my shop. He's got to be honest. No thieves!

ELENA

(*to MARIA*)

He wants somebody to mind the store while he goes
looking for young girls!

GERALDO

I don't look for young girls. I just put myself where
they can find me!

MARIA

Geraldo, you don't need a young man; you need an old
dog. That way you can be the boss and the dog can eat
the terrible food you make.

GERALDO

Be serious, woman. A businessman on the way up
needs an assistant. Somebody with energy, not like
these boys around here.

ELENA

If you paid them a decent wage, they would have
energy. You rob people without a gun, *diablo viejo*!

GERALDO

So what's better, a little money or no money? You tell
me that. If I pay *one* dollar an hour, it's better than *no*
dollars an hour. I'm a poor man trying to feed the good
people in this neighborhood.

MARIA
In the restaurant, you're a poor man, Geraldo. But you
do all right with the poker games in the back room.

SEVERAL OF THE RESIDENTS
ALL *RIGHT*!

GERALDO laughs.

ELENA
What's the boy got to do?

GERALDO
(*suddenly serious*)
He has to make enchiladas, corn dogs, hot dogs,
chicken wings, and whatever else I say. And it all
has to be gourmet.

ELENA
Geraldo, you are *loco*. Totally crazy.

ANGEL, a young man who's been hanging out nearby, sidles up to them.

ANGEL
(*opening his jacket to reveal a row of watches*)
Hey, anybody want to buy a good watch? Cheap, man.
Twenty-four-karat gold, real diamonds. Fifteen dollars.

GERALDO

I already have two watches. Both are five minutes fast.

ANGEL

These are five minutes slow, *papi*. That's a sign. You can't pass up one of these.

JUAN, an older man, has been sitting on a bench nearby.

JUAN

What do you need two watches for? Around here nobody is in a hurry. If you got nothing to do, you only need one watch.

JIMENEZ and CARLOS, the domino players, both stand up at once.

JIMENEZ

You can't take a move back! Once your finger comes off the piece, you can't take it back!

CARLOS

I didn't take my finger off the piece. I had my finger on it, and you moved it to see what I was doing!

JIMENEZ

We're playing for fifty cents! You can't cover up your moves. You think I just fell off the cart and I'm going to let you cover up your moves?

ELENA
(*to JIMENEZ*)
He can't hear you. You have to holler into his good ear.

JIMENEZ
I said you can't be covering up your moves!

Suddenly, sirens and flashing lights signal the arrival of the police. No one seems alarmed, though they know enough to stay in place. CARLOS takes something from his pocket and tosses it into a nearby trash can.

A team of street-duty POLICE OFFICERS, including OFFICERS SHEA and LANE, assembles quickly from either side of the stage. ZUNIGA, the police sergeant, directs his men around the stage, all facing the rear. Then, satisfied that the men are in place, he approaches the door of the apartment building next to Delgado's and knocks boldly as the other officers aim their guns menacingly. TÍA SOFIA, a remarkably attractive older woman dressed in a housecoat and curlers, answers the door.

ZUNIGA
Police! Stand aside.

TÍA SOFIA
(*defiantly*)
Do you have a search warrant? Let me see it!

ZUNIGA
(*turning slightly*)
The warrant!

The other officers look around to see who has brought the warrant, but, to their embarrassment, it is not found.

ZUNIGA

What the hell is wrong with you people? Keep your guns ready. I'll call headquarters!

ZUNIGA goes to one side and radios headquarters. The other officers relax.

TÍA SOFIA
(to the crowd)

They come to search our place, but they don't have a warrant! No warrant, no searching! Who do they think they are? This is America!

There are cries of approval and general laughter from the street residents.

JIMENEZ

They watch too much television. That's why they're taking time out for a commercial.

ZUNIGA

Put your teeth in when you talk to me, lover boy.

OFFICER SHEA
(to ELENA)

Why don't you come home with me? You would look good on my sofa.

ELENA
(*touching SHEA's ears*)
Ah, still wet. I thought so. Come back when you've
grown up, *papi*.

The other OFFICERS laugh.

*MICAELA enters from stage right. She is wearing a blue plaid jumper,
which is significantly less flamboyant than the outfits worn by the
other women of the block. She looks at the women wearing tight pants
and short skirts. Then she begins looking at the POLICE OFFICERS,
obviously searching for someone.*

MICAELA
(*to SHEA*)
Do you know José? He's on the force. Is he with you?
Sometimes they call him DJ.

ZUNIGA
(*who has overheard MICAELA*)
I know him. Sure. He's not here yet. But he'll be here
soon. He's bringing the warrant. You want to sit in the
car with me? Get out of the hot sun?

He tries to put his arm around MICAELA, who slips easily away.

MICAELA
No, it's all right.

ZUNIGA
Hey, don't fly away so soon, little bird.

MICAELA
I'll come back after a while. You sure he's coming here?

ZUNIGA
Any minute. This is a rough neighborhood. Come with me, and I'll protect you. What's your name?

MICAELA
Micaela. I'm a friend of José's. Tell him his friend—the teacher's aide—was looking for him. He'll know who I am.

She leaves, looking cautiously around the neighborhood as she does.

ZUNIGA watches MICAELA go and then turns back toward the old lady in the doorway.

ZUNIGA
(to the OFFICERS, pointing to TÍA SOFIA)
Keep an eye on that one!

TÍA SOFIA
(tossing the front of her dress up)
And don't forget to read me my rights!

OFFICER LANE
Look—here's José now.

ZUNIGA
Men! Fall in! Get ready!

The men get ready to enter the building as JOSÉ approaches. JOSÉ goes directly to ZUNIGA and whispers something in his ear that clearly disturbs the sergeant.

ZUNIGA
What do you mean, we have to go to the judge again? What happened to the warrant we had before? By the time we go through the whole process, they'll have moved their operation to another building!

JOSÉ
What can I tell you?

ZUNIGA
I'll call the captain. By the way, there was a girl looking for you. Okay-looking, not from around here, I think.

JOSÉ
Dark hair? Pretty?

ZUNIGA
Aren't they all?

TÍA SOFIA
(calling from the doorway)
Who's the captain? Tell him Sofia says hello.

ZUNIGA, on the side, gesticulates as he talks into the radio. We can't hear his conversation but see that he is upset.

ZUNIGA
(angrily)
The operation is off! Get the men out of here! How are we going to shut down *anything* with this stupid paperwork?

A loud buzzing noise comes from the factory. Instantly the younger men in the area jump to their feet. One, MANNY, begins to brush off his jacket. Another, GATO, first pulls up his pants, then lowers them to just the right height to be cool.

ZUNIGA
What's that? Their all-clear signal?

OFFICER LANE
Lunchtime at the factory!

The door of Delgado's opens, and the factory girls come out, strutting and chatting. Many are on cell phones, and most are speaking a combination of English and Spanish. Among the girls is FRASQUITA, who has a fair complexion and light brown eyes. She is wearing a tight blouse and even tighter jeans.

As the girls strut, the boys hover around. Music begins and slowly the posturing changes into a formal dance. We see the boys, who were nondescript at first, slowly change into gentlemen, proud of their heritage and respectful of the women. Then we hear the music of "El Ritmo del Barrio." 𝄞

The cops watch, putting away their guns as the lights transform the dingy buildings into glowing neighborhood edifices. ZUNIGA leans against a pole, eyeing the girls.

As the dance ends . . .

ZUNIGA

Why don't you young ladies come to the precinct with us? The afternoon is young, and we can dance. I have a few moves I can show you.

OFFICER SHEA
(*to FRASQUITA*)

Hey, beautiful, you married, or you waiting for me?

FRASQUITA

Married? You need two things to get married. Do you know what they are?

OFFICER SHEA
(*proudly*)

A wedding ring and a license!

FRASQUITA

No, white boy. A passport and a job. No passport and you can't stay here. No job, and there's no love. Not from this girl!

OFFICER LANE
(*to SHEA*)

These girls are nice, but I heard they've got somebody special here. They call her Carmen. I don't know what she looks like, but they say she's hot.

OFFICER SHEA

Ya seen one, ya seen them all.

Suddenly the door to Delgado's opens again, and a stunning young woman commands the space of the doorway. It is CARMEN. She is dressed in a white blouse, a short bolero jacket, and a black skirt. Her mirrored sunglasses reflect the afternoon heat. A flower sticks out from under the jaunty cap she wears, but the most amazing thing about her is the smile she flashes ever so briefly.

OFFICER LANE

Wait—there she is! Oh, my God! Is she fine or *what?*

CARMEN descends the factory's three front steps like the diva she is. The boys form an open circle in front of her, and she takes her rightful place in its center. Among the boys are MANNY, GATO, and ANGEL.

MANNY
Carmen, I'm yours forever!

GATO
Carmen, it's me who is in love with you. I've always been in love with you.

ANGEL
(*sinking to his knees*)
You finally found me. Now tell these fools who you really love so they can die in peace.

CARMEN
Get off your knees, handsome. People will think you're serious.

GATO
Serious enough to marry you this very moment, Carmen.

FRASQUITA
All they know is push-push, Carmen. They don't know about real love.

CARMEN
They know about love, Frasquita. But they still think it's for us, that love is going to come flying down this street. Love isn't coming to this neighborhood.

FRASQUITA

Unless it finds its way to flicker across the television screens or in the movies.

CARMEN

What are all of these cops here for?

ANGEL

They were going to raid Tía Sofia's place, but they forgot the warrant. She ain't letting nobody in without a warrant.

CARMEN
(*looking at JOSÉ*)

Frasquita, I know that guy over there. The one with his hat off. We used to live on the same block when I was a kid.

FRASQUITA

He's tall.

One of the factory girls, MERCEDES, thin and chesty and working her high heels, comes over.

MERCEDES

What's going down?

FRASQUITA

There was supposed to be a raid, but the cops blew it. Now they're standing around, trying to figure out what to do. Carmen used to date the guy leaning against the car.

MERCEDES

You dated a cop?

CARMEN

I didn't say I dated him. I said we used to live on the same block. He's about four years older than me. I had a crush on him.

FRASQUITA

I was in love with an older guy once. I would have married him but his wife was my cousin, so . . .

MERCEDES

Anyway, you can't be in love with a cop. Cops don't have hearts. They got little tin badges inside where their hearts should be.

CARMEN

I was in love with him once. A little.

FRASQUITA

And what did he say when you told him?

CARMEN

I never told him. Maybe I should now.

MERCEDES

Hey, wait a minute. Do you know who that guy is? I saw his picture in the paper. He's the one who shot that kid in the park. He could be weird. You don't want to fall for a guy like that.

CARMEN

Girlfriend, I don't "fall" for nobody. I'm not into love games anymore. I know what love is all about, and this girl is staying on the sidelines with her heart under lock and key.

FRASQUITA

Lock and key!

CARMEN

(*sings "La Habanera"*) 𝄞

Love is a bird that sweetly dreams,
Soaring high in a clear blue sky.
He wants to rest, to settle down,
But summer comes and he has to fly.

You call to me; I turn away,
But I listen as sweet love sings.
I want to go, I want to stay,
While within me, my heart has wings.
L'amour, L'amour, L'amour, L'amour . . .

Latino boys have love so true,
But in my heart I must always be free.
You ignore me, then I'll love you,
And when I do, beware of me.

You ignore me—at least you'll try,
But I'll love you,
And if I love you, if I love you,
Beware of me!

20 ～

Act I. Scene 1.

FRASQUITA

Carmen is right! Love is not for us!

CARMEN
(looking at JOSÉ)

I bet he doesn't even remember me. I think I was ten when he moved.

MERCEDES

Ten? Carmen, you were never ten! Anyway, boys don't remember anything.

CARMEN

You're right. I'll say hello, anyway.

CARMEN goes over to JOSÉ, who is looking at some papers. She puts her hand over the papers, and he looks up.

CARMEN

José Ibarra. You know I remember you from the old neighborhood, when I lived on Manhattan Avenue. You lived in the only building on the block with an elevator.

JOSÉ

That was a long time ago.

CARMEN

You used to buy potato chips from Ferrara's and eat them on the corner. Once I was standing in the

doorway of my building and when I saw you passing,
I lifted my skirt a little so you could see my legs. You
didn't even look in my direction.

JOSÉ
We were both young. You're very pretty now.

CARMEN
You went to church with your mother every Sunday.
The early Mass.

JOSÉ
You were really watching me.

CARMEN
De pe a pa. We were poor, and you looked rich. We were
nothing much, and you looked pretty special to me.

JOSÉ
You know, I remember you now. Someone said you
were a gypsy.

CARMEN
You don't remember me.

JOSÉ
Didn't you go to Saint Dominic's? But you were just
a kid.

CARMEN

(*smiling as she twirls*)

Am I a kid now?

CARMEN dances playfully around JOSÉ. The other cops motion for him to go after her, but he tries to ignore her. Finally, he takes a step toward her, but she moves quickly away. She stops, takes the flower from her hair, and tosses it to him. He catches the flower and looks down at it as she crosses toward him.

JOSÉ

For me?

CARMEN

For you, baby. I didn't know you would still be so handsome. Your wife must be proud of you.

JOSÉ

I don't have a wife.

CARMEN

Then your woman must be happy with you.

JOSÉ

I don't ... What do you care?

CARMEN

I care about a lot of things. You'd be surprised.

CARMEN moves closer to JOSÉ. The other cops gesture for him to go after her, but he is shy. When he takes another step toward her, she runs away and into Delgado's as the other officers laugh.

ZUNIGA
Okay, okay, let's get back to the station. We've got work to do.

TÍA SOFIA
And don't come back without a warrant!

ZUNIGA
In this neighborhood, nobody has an education and everybody is a lawyer!

MERCEDES
In this neighborhood, you don't need an education because they don't hire us anyway. You need to be a lawyer because one way or another—you will get arrested.

ZUNIGA
Yeah, yeah. Look, *mami*, we don't need your lectures today. When we come back, we'll arrest you first.

MERCEDES
Oooooh, Officer, I'm sooo scared!

MERCEDES follows the other factory girls from Delgado's back to work.

The POLICE OFFICERS begin to pack it in, gathering their gear and leaving in twos and threes. MICAELA comes from around a corner.

ZUNIGA
José, what are you now? The village stud? First Carmen gives you the eye, and now this girl comes to look for you again. She was here before.

JOSÉ
What girl?

He sees MICAELA and smiles broadly, putting the flower that CARMEN gave him into his pocket.

MICAELA
I was looking for you.

JOSÉ
And here I am. How are you?

ZUNIGA and other officers are off to one side, leaving JOSÉ and MICAELA center stage.

MICAELA
I'm good. I like working at the school. The hours are good, and the pay's all right. I'm taking classes in the summer. Maybe I can get a degree and teach.

JOSÉ

Sounds good to me. What are you doing in this neighborhood?

MICAELA

I told your mother I was coming over here today to the new Lowe's to buy a picture frame. She gave me a message for you.

JOSÉ

How is she?

MICAELA

She misses you. But José, she's so happy. She's finally been accepted into the senior citizen housing. One bedroom and one and a half baths. The building is beautiful, overlooking the park. She gave me this letter for you. She asked me to ...

MICAELA blushes as she looks away.

JOSÉ

To what?

MICAELA

She kissed me and asked me to pass it on to you.

JOSÉ
Well, if she asked you to pass it on, you can't keep it for
yourself....

MICAELA shyly kisses JOSÉ.

MICAELA
And here's the letter. She was hoping you would call
more often. I can understand that.

JOSÉ
I'm glad she's moving, but I have so many good
memories of that small apartment we lived in. We
would sit in the kitchen, with the sun beaming
through the fragile white curtains. All of life was before
us then. There was nothing but hope and the promise
of good things to come.

MICAELA
You think of your mother, your home.... You are so
sweet, José. Maybe one day...

JOSÉ
What does she say in the letter?

MICAELA
(*anxious to leave before he reads it*)
I have to go. You can read it later.

JOSÉ

Stay a minute. I haven't seen you in weeks.

MICAELA

I have to go. Really. I would ... I would like to see more of you.

She starts to leave, pauses for a moment to take a last look at JOSÉ, then exits.

JOSÉ
(reading the letter)

"Dear Son, I hope this letter finds you well. I have sent it by Micaela, who has been so helpful to me. José, if you want, you can move into my old apartment, the one you loved so much as a child. It has two bedrooms, as you remember, big enough to start a family. I will be so glad when you marry. I know that once you marry, you will be more careful, even if you remain a policeman. I hope you find someone who will love you. Someone like Micaela. You know she loves you almost as much as I do. Your loving mother."

I want to make my mother happy, to make her a grandmother and see the smile on her face as she plays with the children. And she's right: Micaela does care a lot for me, and she's a solid girl. Nothing flighty about her. Her working at the school is good, too.

There is the sound of fighting offstage, and a glass vase comes flying out of one of the factory's windows.

ZUNIGA

What the—? Shea, Lane, go into that building to see what's going on!

SHEA and LANE enter Delgado's, guns drawn.

ZUNIGA

This place is a hellhole. Useless people doing useless things. Wasting their time.

TÍA SOFIA

All they have to spend is their time. So they do it freely.

ZUNIGA

What? You haven't died yet? What are you waiting for?

TÍA SOFIA

For you to die first so I can pee on your grave!

ZUNIGA

If I ever get the chance to arrest you, you old hag, I'll handcuff you to a fire hydrant and leave you there!

TÍA SOFIA

Hey, how did you get to be so ugly? You take pills for that, or what?

ZUNIGA

Shut up!

TÍA SOFIA

Just tell me one thing and I'll shut up. Did your father have a tail?

ZUNIGA reaches for his gun as TÍA SOFIA slams her door shut.

OFFICERS SHEA and LANE come out of Delgado's with half of the factory workers, including FRASQUITA, all shouting about who started the fight. In the middle, held by SHEA and LANE, is a very angry CARMEN.

ZUNIGA

What happened?

OFFICER SHEA

A fight broke out between this one and another girl.

FRASQUITA

The other girl started it! She said that Carmen had a big mouth!

CARMEN

And all I said was that the flies like her mouth because her breath smells like—

ZUNIGA

I don't want to hear this nonsense!

CARMEN

Neither do I! Let's send out for pizza!

ZUNIGA

You keep your mouth shut. Shea, is this serious?

OFFICER SHEA

The other girl has a cut across her face. And this one had a knife.

ZUNIGA

(*to CARMEN*)

What did you do? Cut her?

CARMEN

(*singing flightily*)

Did I? Could I? I'm not talking!

Hands behind her back, CARMEN dances around ZUNIGA.

ZUNIGA

Don't play with me, Carmen. Now tell me what happened in there.

CARMEN

(*still singing*)

Burn me! Torture me! I'm not talking! Tra la la, tra la la, tra la la la la la la la la la!

ZUNIGA

José, handcuff her and take her in. We'll show these people we're not playing!

ZUNIGA and the other men start off. JOSÉ has handcuffed CARMEN, who looks over her shoulder at him.

CARMEN

The handcuffs are too tight!

JOSÉ

They're not tight at all.

CARMEN

Not for you, of course. You're a big, strong man, but I'm just a helpless woman. How tall are you, anyway? Seven feet? Look how strong your arms are, and how long. You can put one of your arms completely around my body!

She spins into his arms.

JOSÉ

Behave yourself! You brought this on yourself.

CARMEN

How can you do this to a fellow Italian?

JOSÉ

You're not Italian, and neither am I.

CARMEN

How can you tell I'm not Italian?

JOSÉ

Your dark eyes tell me that you're Latina. Your accent is
Dominican, and your lips . . .
                    (*stopping himself*)
Well, you're quite attractive.

CARMEN

Oh, Officer José, tell me what my lips say to you.
Whisper it to me. But hold me close so I can hear you.

JOSÉ

Look, you're going to jail! Don't talk to me.

CARMEN

Oh, you've got me too excited. I need a drink.
Something cool. I have a friend who owns a club.

JOSÉ

I told you to keep quiet.

CARMEN

Why are you so hard on me? Don't you remember me?
I'm the little gypsy girl who lifted her dress so you
could see her legs, remember? I was in love with you,
and you just glanced at me coldly because I was so ugly.

JOSÉ
(weakening)

You weren't ugly.

CARMEN

And skinny.

JOSÉ

You were thin.

CARMEN

And now? Still too ugly? Still too thin? Wait—let me lift my skirt up....

CARMEN touches the hem of her skirt but doesn't lift it.

JOSÉ

Carmen!

CARMEN

We can meet at my friend's club. You'll love him. It has lots of corners. We can sit and look into each other's eyes.

JOSÉ

Don't talk to me like that. I'm a police officer!

CARMEN

Okay, and I'm just a prisoner. And I'm afraid, so I'll sing to myself. I always sing to myself when I'm afraid. As I am now.

She hums "La Seguidilla."

JOSÉ
(weakening more)

This isn't right.

CARMEN

We can make it right!

JOSÉ

You don't mean what you say! You're just . . .

CARMEN

A girl trapped by a huge man who has her in his power. Whose heart is beating wildly as he towers over her! But instead of just feeling fear, she is beginning to have deeper feelings for him. I'm that little girl again in the old neighborhood. Not knowing if I can even go there again. Not knowing if that place even exists anymore.

JOSÉ
(weakening further)

Do you want that place to exist again?

CARMEN

I'm too embarrassed to say what I *really* want, José.

CARMEN dances in front of JOSÉ, handcuffed hands behind her,
pushing them toward him. Finally, he unlocks them. CARMEN turns
and takes JOSÉ's face in her hands as if to kiss him, then pushes him
away and runs. She stops at the far end of the stage.

JOSÉ

Don't make fun of me, Carmen.

CARMEN

No, it's my heart that's making fun of me. Leading
me into love again when I'm so afraid of it. I'm not
laughing at you, José. I would never do that.

JOSÉ

I came here a shell, wondering about my career, and
my life. Now you've found all the empty spaces and
filled them.

CARMEN

If I escape, will you be too angry to ever see me again?
Or will you wonder how I would feel if I were in your
arms, the way I am wondering how it would be?

JOSÉ

Carmen ... Carmen ... You make me think too much.
I am drunk with thoughts of you.

CARMEN

Lillas Pastia's club. I'll be waiting for you.

CARMEN rushes to JOSÉ, kisses him passionately, then runs off.
JOSÉ is standing forlornly in the middle of the stage, holding his empty
handcuffs. ZUNIGA appears and looks around for CARMEN. He stares
at JOSÉ, hands uplifted in question. He sees JOSÉ's shoulders droop and
understands what has happened. Then he crosses the stage and stares
directly into the JOSÉ's face. JOSÉ turns slowly away, cringing.
ZUNIGA turns to SHEA and LANE and motions them over.

ZUNIGA

This is what happens to weak men. He's let that girl get
away. Write him up. I'll do the rest. He doesn't deserve
to be in our unit.

Embarrassed, SHEA and LANE walk away after ZUNIGA.

For a moment the stage is empty except for JOSÉ and some neighborhood
types, who are motionless. Then an old man enters from stage right,
pushing a cart. Perched on the cart is a portable radio that plays the
"Destiny Theme." 𝄞

Scene 2

We are at Lillas Pastia's social club. It is modest, with a roped-off area and a small, slightly raised stage. CARMEN is sitting at a table with MERCEDES and FRASQUITA. Several people are standing at the bar, most sipping small cups of coffee or tea.

FRASQUITA

Carmen, look at you! You're glowing! Are you sick?

MERCEDES

(feeling CARMEN's forehead)

She's got the flu!

CARMEN

I feel fine!

FRASQUITA

You're depressed. Tell me what's on your mind. It's better to get it off your chest.

CARMEN

What's on my mind? I'm thinking about a certain police officer. Six feet tall ... dark eyes ...

MERCEDES

(*alarmed*)

Oh, my God! She's in love.

FRASQUITA

With a policeman? Not that José? I don't believe it.

CARMEN

Little scraggly mustache . . .

MERCEDES

Carmen, please tell me you are not in love with any
man. Then tell me two times that you are not even
thinking of being in love with a cop!

FRASQUITA

She's thinking of it. Even though she knows that love
doesn't work these streets. When love has to pass
through *el barrio*, it takes a taxi.

MERCEDES

And keeps its head down so it won't even see us.

FRASQUITA

Then sneaks away without paying! How do you know
you're in love? It could be swine flu.

CARMEN

I just keep thinking about him, Frasquita. He's like a
tune I can't get out of my head.

MERCEDES

Carmen, you of all people. You know better. He'll
forget your face and your eyes and your heart. All he'll
see is another poor Latina longing for a life she can't
have. Love is for people with bank accounts. And
besides, if he felt *that* much for you, he'd be around
here looking for you. When did you see him last?

CARMEN

They put him on loan to the tunnel authority. All day
long he has to breathe car exhaust. It's only temporary.

FRASQUITA

Temporary? They're going to move the tunnel?

CARMEN

No, the assignment. His sergeant is mad because I
got away.

MERCEDES

Frasquita's right. Love isn't for poor people, honey. You
show me a man without a job or a kicking hustle, and
I'll show you a dude that's mad at the world. We're just
sweet meat if a man can't afford to get married. For us
it's just a quick kiss, a quick hug—

FRASQUITA

A quick bam-bam-bam—

MERCEDES

And a long, sad time to think about it later. You know too much to believe in fairy tales, Carmen.

CARMEN

My head knows who I am, Frasquita. My head tells me, *"¡Vamos, chica!"* But my heart says, "Hey, Carmencita, maybe this time it'll work out."

MERCEDES

The last time he saw you he arrested you!

CARMEN

And let me go! This time he will come and maybe he'll put me up against the wall.

FRASQUITA

That he might do.

CARMEN sits on a table, hands between her knees.

CARMEN

He'll run his hands over my body, looking for weapons, and I'll tell him all the places he's missing. Then he'll notice that my heart is beating fast, and he'll ask me what I have to fear if I'm telling him the truth. I'll tell

him I think I'm having a heart attack, and he'll have
to put his ear to my chest to listen to the rhythm. . . .

MERCEDES

She's really in love.

CARMEN

Then he'll see that I'm trembling and put his arms
around me.

FRASQUITA

And suddenly all the streets with the empty food
wrappers and the potholes and the garbage will
disappear and you'll be in a gleaming white castle
on a hill far away. . . .

CARMEN

It could happen. I feel it in my bones. There's
something about him, something that draws me
to him. That excites me, too. You don't like him?

MERCEDES

I guess he's all right. I like men, too, but I only like
them for a little while. Two weeks, three, unless there's
a holiday coming up. You have to stay with them
through the holidays.

CARMEN

He makes me feel like a schoolgirl again.

MERCEDES
That's *good* to you? Why? I don't remember you doing any dancing on the way to school.

CARMEN
You're getting to be too hard.

FRASQUITA
Or you're getting to be too soft!

CARMEN
Maybe, Frasquita. Maybe I'm too soft and he's too romantic. I know.

MERCEDES
Your head knows, but your heart is too crazy to listen.

FRASQUITA
You got to be careful, homegirl. You open your heart, and it's more dangerous than opening your legs.

CARMEN
What don't I know?

MERCEDES
(*resigned*)
It's wonderful, Carmen. Good luck with this dude.

FRASQUITA

Yeah, it's wonderful.

The three girls, knowing what a momentous decision CARMEN is making, embrace one another.

On the small stage, a guitarist picks up his instrument and slowly plucks the same "Destiny Theme" we heard earlier. ♪

MERCEDES

Whoa! What is that tune? Is there a funeral? Play something with life to it!

The guitarist quickly switches to something much livelier. Several patrons enter, including GERALDO, OFFICER SHEA, and SERGEANT ZUNIGA.

GERALDO

Cold drinks for the ladies over there.

BARTENDER

Six dollars!

GERALDO

Six dollars? You selling blood? What do you mean, robbing people like that?

ZUNIGA

I can afford it. Three drinks for the lovely ladies.

FRASQUITA
Keep your drinks! I'm not thirsty.

ZUNIGA
They'll keep you cool. You look like a hot mama to me.

FRASQUITA
And you look old and cold to me.

ZUNIGA
You'd be surprised, *chica*!

MERCEDES
Chica? Now you're acting Latino? I don't *think* so.

OFFICER SHEA
What would you like us to be?

CARMEN
Gone! That's what we would like you to be.

OFFICER SHEA
She's longing for José. He makes her blood boil. He's good with these locals.

MERCEDES
Local? I don't go *local*, but I will go *loca* on your skinny butt!

ZUNIGA

José's a loser. We've got him sucking fumes on traffic duty.

OFFICER SHEA

He's back on the beat today. Maybe he can find somebody else to turn loose.

CARMEN

(*perking up*)

He's back? Today?

ZUNIGA

(*edging closer to CARMEN*)

Look, you can do better than that guy.

FRASQUITA

Man, you really think you're hot stuff, don't you?

ZUNIGA

I've been around. I know how to make a girl like Carmen happy. Maybe I'll take her shopping. Bet you would like that, eh, Carmen?

CARMEN

Cierra el pico, man, because ain't nothing coming out that I want to hear.

ZUNIGA

I know what I have to know. You're straight street, and
I know how to take care of you.

FRASQUITA

Go home and take care of your wife.

MERCEDES
(*looking at her watch*)
He can't go home yet. His wife's boyfriend is still there
having dinner.

The girls all laugh.

*Suddenly we hear a commotion. A PATRON gets off his stool,
shrugs to the crowd, and goes to the door. He looks out.*

PATRON

It's Escamillo!

MERCEDES

Here?

FRASQUITA

He's going to shoot a video in the neighborhood. It
was in the papers.

*ESCAMILLO enters. The one-time street rapper turned entrepreneur
and film producer fits the description often ascribed to him as the richest*

man ever to come out of Spanish Harlem. Tall and broad-shouldered, *he's wearing a light-gray tailored Italian suit with a sky-blue shirt. Over his shoulders is a satin silver-gray cape that shimmers as he walks. As he enters, he hands his assistant, GORDITO, his walking stick and hesitates just inside the doorway as one of his bodyguards removes the cape.*

GORDITO takes center stage and begins framing film shots with his hands as ESCAMILLO leans casually against the bar.

GORDITO
(raps)

Hey, Escamillo can lift this place from its obscurity
And bring it to a place of peace and security
With a slam bam jam that opens the dam of go and flow,
But he needs something real to express how he feels
As a master blaster lifting his fate above the disaster
Of free-floating hate, and if your brain has the uplift
To master the hard drift from grime to sublime,
He might give you some time and ... *who knows?*

He puts his hand to his ear.

MERCEDES

Who knows?

GORDITO

Even a 3-D flick! Let me step aside for the pride of San Juan, Santo Domingo, México, Bogotá, and El Bronx Remembered! Escamillo!

WALTER DEAN MYERS

ESCAMILLO
I said *what?* I said *what?* I said WHAT'S HAPPENING?

FRASQUITA
Yo, Escamillo! Put me in a movie. The world needs to
see me.

*In the background, we hear the strains of "The Toreador Song" 𝄞,
rhythmic and upbeat, which continue as Escamillo speaks.*

ESCAMILLO
(begins rapping)
The world needs to see all of us, *mis amigos*. That's what
Escamillo is all about. Fighting against the invisibility
of being poor, being a nobody. They don't kill us! They
don't lynch us! They make us invisible, as if we don't
really exist! They take away our identity. At first we think
it's harmless; we just don't see ourselves anywhere.
We see shells where men should be standing; we see
cartoons where our women should be. But then one
day you wake up and look in the mirror, and there's no
one there looking back at you. All the dreams that held
you together are gone, and all the hope you could feel is
gone. You know your brain is fading fast and you feel a
sense of panic.

Invisibility sees your panic, smells your despair as it paws
the ground waiting to charge across the arena, waiting
to destroy you. But now ESCAMILLO has given you the

warning, and you are ready to fight back. The cold steel of truth is in your hand and you get ready. Across from you, invisibility trots proudly, snorting its contempt for you.

Okay, my people. Show me what you got!

The club suddenly comes alive as the patrons begin to dance. The dancing ranges from salsa to a kind of street flamenco. ESCAMILLO nods approvingly as he sees the vibrant life of the community. But throughout the dancing, CARMEN sits at the far end of the bar, looking on with apparent disinterest.

ESCAMILLO

Yo, I see the happenings! I feel the beat! I see the beauty and feel the heat! But where are the stars in this tiny universe? Where are the sisters and brothers gonna shoot across the sky? Who's gonna light up the firmament? Where are the heart stoppers? The hammer droppers? Yo, *mamacita*, I see you glowing like you knowing something spelled truth. What's the word, little bird?

CARMEN

I'm not interested in your moves or your movies, Escamillo. And Hollywood is not on my to-do list.

ESCAMILLO

I thought you were special, and I definitely got an eye for fly.

GORDITO

She fades into the woodwork like yesterday's news.

ESCAMILLO

No, Gordito, she ain't fading. She's masquerading
as ordinary, but she looks dangerous to me, and you
know how I flirt with a danger high. It brings out
the bullfighter—the toreador—in me.

*CARMEN lifts her hands to her head, fingers pointed as if to represent
horns, and struts sensuously toward ESCAMILLO, who instantly takes
the challenge and goes into a bull-fighting pose. CARMEN makes three
passes at ESCAMILLO, all of which he sidesteps deftly. Hands on hips,
she throws her head back in laughter. Then she lifts her arms to the
ceiling and swoops them down, jabbing her fingers into ESCAMILLO's
side. She and ESCAMILLO both laugh.*

GORDITO

It's time to go. We have to see the manager before the
concert to iron out last-minute details. And there are a
million dollars in these details. He wants to negotiate
foreign rights and subsidiaries. We have to be there.

ESCAMILLO

Of course. Of course.
         (He takes his cape.)
But I will be back for you. What is your name, angel?

CARMEN

Carmen. Or Carmencita. Your choice.

ESCAMILLO

Carmen. Carmencita. It's all the same. You are too beautiful for words. My tongue gets excited just saying your name. I will be back for you. To everybody here: you are all invited to my concert this weekend. I'll send fifty tickets over to
> *(looks around and sees the sign above the stage)*

Lillas's place.

FRASQUITA

This show is going to be good, right?

ESCAMILLO

The fire department is sending over a special truck, it's going to be so hot.

FRASQUITA

Is it going to be on television? Because when concerts are on television, they're usually pretty good.

ESCAMILLO

This won't be good because of television, baby.
> *(turning to Carmen)*

This is going to be good because of Carmen. Everything I think up I'm going to be asking myself what Carmencita's going to be thinking about it, and then I'm going to make it even better. I'm good whenever I'm awake, but when I got somebody to inspire me, I'm knee-deep in fantastic!

CARMEN

You got game, and you're running it!

ESCAMILLO

Your game is deeper, baby, but Escamillo's steadily climbing on up. I think we just might reach the top together!

CARMEN

I'll be there.

ESCAMILLO

All you need to bring is your heart and your dancing shoes. Leave the rest to Escamillo.

ESCAMILLO and his entourage leave.

MERCEDES

Carmen, he was digging on you something crazy.
No tengas pena just because you're in love.

FRASQUITA

He can take me to Hollywood anytime he wants to, but I'm not doing nothing nasty in front of a camera.

ZUNIGA

(*after ESCAMILLO's people leave*)

That Escamillo's all glitter. Nothing more. No substance. You can dress up street, but you can't take away the stink. Let's get out of here.

ZUNIGA and SHEA leave.

MERCEDES

He's going to go look for somebody else to hate.

CARMEN

He probably hates himself.

The excitement of ESCAMILLO lingers for a while in the air, then slowly dies down as DANCAIRO and RAIMONDO enter. DANCAIRO is thin and nervous and has a teardrop tattoo under his left eye. RAIMONDO is short and heavy, with the nervous habit of hunching his shoulders as he speaks.

RAIMONDO

(*to MERCEDES*)

We got it going. Major-league stuff all the way.

DANCAIRO

We can score every credit card number in the city of Pittsburgh for three hours. That's a hundred and fifty-nine thousand names.

RAIMONDO
And they're rich in Pittsburgh.

DANCAIRO
In three hours, we can make a fortune.

RAIMONDO
And since it's all electronic, there's no evidence.

DANCAIRO
No fingerprints. No DNA. Just get in and boom, boom, boom! It'll take them three hours to figure out what's happening and another three hours to shut the system down, and we'll be done by then.

RAIMONDO
We've got the log-in code. All we need is two smart kids who can hack into one lousy computer to get the master password. Then we're in and gone without even a gun drawn. Thank God for technology.

DANCAIRO
(to *CARMEN*)
And we also need the charms of some beautiful women to keep a certain computer security chief—how do you say?—occupied!

MERCEDES
How much is in it for us?

FRASQUITA
We don't work for nothing!

RAIMONDO
Fifty thousand—twenty-five thousand apiece—if the score is small.

DANCAIRO
I would tell you how much you would get if it is completely successful, but I can't count that high.

FRASQUITA
You got us!

RAIMONDO
Carmen?

MERCEDES
She's too much in love. With a cop!

RAIMONDO
No, I'm serious. Carmen, are you with us?

CARMEN
I've got stuff on my mind, Raimondo. Maybe some other time.

RAIMONDO

What some other time? This is once in a lifetime, sweet cheeks!

MERCEDES

Lighten up, Raimondo. She's got a life, too.

FRASQUITA

(*spots JOSÉ at the door*)

And here he is.

JOSÉ enters. DANCAIRO and RAIMONDO back away quickly, DANCAIRO shielding his face with his hand. They both exit out of the rear door but not before RAIMONDO glances toward CARMEN and shakes his head in disbelief.

JOSÉ

Carmen, I've been looking everywhere for you. I thought you were going to be home.

CARMEN

Too hot in there. I got home last night and a mouse was sitting in the refrigerator!

JOSÉ

A mouse? Oh, that's a joke. Right. At first I couldn't remember the name of this place. But then I did. You've been on my mind all day.

(*looks around*)
Can we go somewhere?

CARMEN

José, I want you to meet my friends. This is Frasquita.

FRASQUITA

Hey, guy.

CARMEN

And this is Mercedes. They're my homegirls.

MERCEDES

What's happening?

JOSÉ

Hello.

*FRASQUITA and MERCEDES retreat to a table, and JOSÉ kisses
CARMEN's hand tenderly.*

JOSÉ

Nice friends.

CARMEN

The kind that look out for you. You know what I mean?

JOSÉ

Yes, I do. I like loyalty in my friends.

CARMEN

Frasquita asked me why I've been talking about you so
much.

JOSÉ

You've been talking about me? What did you say?

CARMEN

That you make me remember the girl I once was, the
girl who believed in every dream that came her way,
who used to roll the top of her skirts up outside of
Saint Dominic's, hoping the boys would notice her.

JOSÉ

You did go to Saint Dom's.

CARMEN

In a way I did. I mean, it was me, but I wasn't who I
am now. I was just a little girl with wide eyes and teeny
boobs. I was maybe softer inside than I am now.

JOSÉ

You are like a breath of fresh air to me, Carmen. My life
has been just stupid for the last few months. First it
was that kid—

CARMEN

I know about that, José. It was in *La Prensa* that you
shot a boy who threatened you. But I know that's not
who you are. I know that.

JOSÉ

It really hurt to see the things they wrote about me in
the papers.

CARMEN

Nobody wants to hurt another person.

JOSÉ

The thing with the boy—it happened so fast.

CARMEN

The thing?

JOSÉ

He came out of the shadows and . . .

CARMEN

(*putting her fingers on his lips*)
Don't talk about it.

JOSÉ

I've been really depressed since it happened. I can't
sleep.

CARMEN

Let's talk about us.

JOSÉ

Last night I tried to make my mind blank, just not
think about anything. Then, in the morning, the air
was all still and I reached over to get a glass of water
and my hand touched the flower you gave me. You
remember the flower?

CARMEN

You kept it? All this time?

JOSÉ

And suddenly the flower was more than just a flower. It
was a promise that your soul had made to mine. I put
the light on and took it in my hand, and the lightness
of it just spoke of you. I put it to my lips and I could
smell it, and it was as if you were near.

CARMEN

You speak very well, José. I've never been that good
with words. They seem to only get in my way.

JOSÉ

Words are only tools, Carmen.

CARMEN, somewhat unsure of what JOSÉ is saying, stands and moves awkwardly away from him. He reaches for her and takes her wrist, and she turns to face him.

CARMEN

Dancing is a tool, too. Let me dance for you!

JOSÉ

Dance?

CARMEN

(brightly, changing the mood)
Yes, you're the hero that kept me out of the slammer,
and I'll dance in your honor!

CARMEN begins to dance for JOSÉ. From time to time, he reaches for her swirling figure, but she moves away from him.

CARMEN

Look at me! Giddy as a schoolgirl. My body wants to move!

JOSÉ

You move your body, but you've captured my soul.
We'll be together from this moment on. From this very
moment. Promise me. As the flower promised me.

CARMEN

(stops dancing and looks at JOSÉ)
José, my friends say that I'm taking a big risk.

JOSÉ
Take it, Carmen. I'm offering you my life.

CARMEN
(*turning slightly away from JOSÉ*)
José, why do you want me?

JOSÉ
Why? How can you ask a question like that? People look at you and they're amazed. You're the brightest star in their universe. People will look at us walking together and wonder what magic I performed to have you on my arm. They'll know that together we're somebody. That we're special.

CARMEN
I don't want to be that special. Just loved, José. I want to run and jump right into forever after. Does that make sense to you?

JOSÉ's cell phone rings.

CARMEN goes over to him and puts her hand over the phone, which he now holds in his hand. JOSÉ turns as he answers the call.

JOSÉ
Yes? . . . Yes? . . . Of course! I'll be there right away, sir.

CARMEN

What are you doing?

JOSÉ

They need me down at headquarters at once. It's a big operation.

CARMEN

But I'm standing here promising you forever, and suddenly the phone rings and forever is put on hold.

JOSÉ
(*checking his gun*)

I have to go. I have no choice.

CARMEN

No choice? One minute you're saying that you have no choice except to love me, and the next...

JOSÉ

This is my job.

CARMEN
(*confused*)

How can you—? Who are you? One minute you're hopelessly in love, and ... and the next minute you're leaving?

JOSÉ
(*roughly*)
Be sensible! I have to go!

CARMEN
(*emulating a ringing phone*)
Brrring! Brrring! Calling all mice! Calling all mice!
Brrring! Brrring! There are crumbs on the carpet for you!

JOSÉ
You don't understand, Carmen.

CARMEN
Yes, yes, you're right. I don't understand. And I don't
understand how I let myself fall in love again! What
was I thinking?

JOSÉ
A man must do his duty, no matter what.

*ZUNIGA enters. He is tipsy. His collar is unbuttoned, and he is carrying
a brown paper bag that probably holds a bottle of liquor.*

ZUNIGA
Carmen! I thought you might still be here. I was
thinking about you all evening. Come sit with me. You
old enough to drink wine? We could go someplace.

JOSÉ
Carmen doesn't need a drink from you.

ZUNIGA turns slowly and eyes JOSÉ with contempt.

ZUNIGA
You still running around the city? When's your hearing? Next week? Then you'll be gone from the force forever, and maybe they can even give you some jail time for letting a prisoner escape. They'll love you on the cell block. Now, get back to the precinct. They must have some wastebaskets that need to be emptied.

He puts his arm around CARMEN.

JOSÉ
(*angrily*)
Don't tell me what to do! I am as much man as you are!

Curious about the shouting, DANCAIRO, RAIMONDO, and ANGEL enter from the back room.

ZUNIGA
(*shouting*)
You? A man? You're a boy who occasionally dresses in the uniform of a man. Now, get out of here before I lose my temper!

WALTER DEAN MYERS

JOSÉ

Go ahead: lose it!

ZUNIGA slaps JOSÉ, and for a minute the two men grapple. Then ZUNIGA throws JOSÉ to the ground.

ZUNIGA

Look at you! Lying on the floor like the child you are!
See how all your friends stare at you—wondering if
you have the nerve to stand up again.

CARMEN
(*to both men*)

Stop it! What are you doing?

JOSÉ
(*pulls out his gun*)

Watch your mouth, man!

ZUNIGA

Why, you going to mug me, lover boy?

JOSÉ fires, and ZUNIGA stiffens as he is grazed in the arm, then draws his own weapon.

CARMEN
(*to JOSÉ*)
Oh, my God! What have you done? We're not
murderers, you fool! Put that gun away!

RAIMONDO rushes over to ZUNIGA and gently pushes his gun down as
DANCAIRO signals JOSÉ to calm down.

RAIMONDO
Sergeant, twenty thousand dollars! You forget this
whole incident, and I'll bring twenty thousand in
small bills. I can have the money by noon tomorrow.
Come on, man. You've taken money before. This is
twenty thousand!

ZUNIGA
(*angry but still greedy*)
Twenty thousand dollars. Small bills. I'll forget this
incident but not this fool! No way I forget him.

DANCAIRO and RAIMONDO escort ZUNIGA out.

JOSÉ
(*standing*)
What have I done? My career is finished.

CARMEN

You shoot a man because he disses you? How stupid
is that? I look at you and I don't know who you are!
When I saw your picture in the paper, I thought I
recognized someone from when I was a girl. But
now I don't recognize you at all!

JOSÉ

Oh, God! Look, Carmen, I love you, but right now I
have to think. I just know my career is wrecked.

CARMEN

What did the *boy* do? Did he look at you wrong, too?

JOSÉ

What boy? Look, I don't have time to talk now. I have
to go and pack some things.
          (*He looks around.*)
I guess I'm one of you now. Carmen, wait here for me!

*JOSÉ leaves, stopping for a moment to look at RAIMONDO as he
returns.*

RAIMONDO

We're screwed if Zuniga changes his mind. He can
arrest everybody here and make it stick if he wants
to. Now we have to pull this job off. We better make
it pay big-time or we're all in trouble. How about you,
Carmen? You down with us now?

CARMEN

Yeah, I'm down, Raimondo. I got nothing to lose.

RAIMONDO

Good. I need to hit the streets and get our lookouts
on the corners in case Zuniga changes his mind and
wants to hit us. You okay, Carmencita?

CARMEN

I'm okay, Raimondo.

RAIMONDO

Everybody out. I need you all on the corners looking
out for the heat. Everybody out!

They all leave except for CARMEN, who stands alone, forlorn.

*CARMEN sits and, for a long beat, thinks about what has happened. We
hear the sound of a harp introducing her song.*

WALTER DEAN MYERS

CARMEN

(sings "Love Has Flown Away") 𝄞

Love came easy, but it just wasn't for me.

It flew away like swallows on a summer evening.

Love sang softly, but it just wasn't to me.

Was I a fool to give my love, to give my soul,

    and more away?

My heart aches with longing, cries each night,

As I just fall apart.

(clearly distressed)

What have I done? What have I done?

Am I so hungry for love that I can't see

It's not going to ever happen for me?

I saw the darkness in his eyes

And knew there was even more darkness

    behind those lovely eyes

And yet . . .

And yet I kept stumbling blindly

Like some silly schoolgirl from another place,

    another time.

I've got to be the old Carmen again.

Too hard to hurt, too hard to fall in love.

The music continues softly as CARMEN puts her head down on the table.

Act Two

Scene 1

We are in the back room of Lillas Pastia's club, which is the home base of DANCAIRO's crew. There is a bar at the back of the stage, and the back wall is covered with colored curtains depicting scenes from a tropical location.

At one table we see CARMEN, FRASQUITA, and MERCEDES. At the end of the bar, JOSÉ is drinking by himself, head down. The atmosphere is fairly busy, and the music from the sound system is upbeat.

MERCEDES

This boy wants me *sooo* much, you wouldn't believe it. If I walk into a room where he is, his heart starts beating faster. You can tell from across the room—you can almost hear it! That's how much he loves me.

FRASQUITA

Is he cute?

MERCEDES

He drives a BMW.

FRASQUITA

That's pretty cute. What was he arrested for?

MERCEDES

How do you know he was arrested? You don't know that.

FRASQUITA

He's young, he lives around here, he's been arrested. What for?

MERCEDES

On a technicality. They caught him with some television sets, which he was going to sell but they got to him before he could get the sets out. Then—and you're not going to believe this—they charged him with *possession* of stolen goods, and the only reason he had them in his possession was because they arrested him before he could sell them!

FRASQUITA

That's got to be some kind of violation. That's what they do to us and then they say we don't have family values. How are we going to have family values when you can't afford a place to put your family?

CARMEN

I think I need somebody new to fall in love with. Maybe this weekend. Any parties going on?

FRASQUITA

Whoa, Carmen. What happened to José? I thought

you were all hot and bothered over him. All the pain in his eyes and everything? I thought you went for that big-time?

CARMEN

Frasquita, I don't know if I was really seeing his pain or just seeing the place where it should have been. Sometimes I look at him and I see that shining knight I was talking about. Then I look again and there's a shadow across his face. I think you can hold some things in you too long and they go bad. It's as if your soul gets dark. Then it gets to be dangerous. I'm a little bit afraid of him. Maybe I let my heart get away from me. It won't happen again.

FRASQUITA

I told you that, girlfriend. I've been there once or twice myself. Yeah, me, Frasquita Margarita Ortiz. I've been head-over-heels in love before. Or was it heels over head? Anyway . . . I've been there! But I'm not sure about you, Carmen. You're, like, really messed around over that dude. I can even hear it in your voice.

CARMEN

I'm over him. Love knows how to die.

DANCAIRO enters with RAMI and YOSHIRO. RAMI is a slightly built Indian, and YOSHIRO is stocky and Japanese.

DANCAIRO

Here's my crew! Lay it out for them, guys.

RAMI

This marketing company in Pittsburgh is buying a list of credit-card users. It's a one-time deal; they're going to try to sell audio equipment over the Internet to everyone on the list. But instead of just sending the names and e-mail addresses, the card company sent the numbers, too. They have a good security system, but one computer—

YOSHIRO

On the third floor.

RAMI

It monitors everything. We've hacked the password and can download all the numbers onto a flash drive in—

YOSHIRO

Forty-two seconds.

RAMI

We need three minutes to go up the back elevator, into the office, get in, and download the numbers, and we're out of there!

DANCAIRO

The building is empty on weekends except for a rent-a-
cop who guards the entrance on the first floor. We get
a girl in there who needs directions because she's lost.
Then she sees how handsome the guard is. The other
two girls are lookouts. Any cops passing by won't be
suspicious of two girls standing on the corner.

FRASQUITA

Sounds good to me.

MERCEDES

And when do we get paid?

DANCAIRO

We'll do the caper Saturday morning, sell the numbers
in the afternoon, and you get paid on Sunday
morning. Right after Mass!

*There are high fives all around, and DANCAIRO leads RAMI and
YOSHIRO out. JOSÉ gets up and approaches the girls' table.*

FRASQUITA

Here comes José. You need us to stay?

CARMEN

No, I'll be okay.

MERCEDES
We'll be in the corner. You need us, *mami,* just whistle.

FRASQUITA and MERCEDES retreat to a corner table.

CARMEN
José, you look like shit, man.

JOSÉ
I feel out of place. What's inside me, what's really
me deep inside, is different from what's inside these
people watching the world go by.

CARMEN
We all think we're different, but when it comes around,
we end up needing the same things. Somebody to love
us. Somebody to respect us.

JOSÉ
Zuniga screwed up my career big-time. All the time I
was on traffic duty, I thought about how he was trying
to bring me down. I made myself think about you
to keep him off my mind. He's trying to destroy me.
You're my flower, my promise of life and hope.

CARMEN
José, I'm not a flower. I'm not a promise. I'm Carmen.

JOSÉ

That's not how I thought of you during those hard
days.

CARMEN

José, you're making my head spin. What else were you
thinking about?

JOSÉ

About my mother, and how much I miss the life I had
with her. Does that sound weak to you? That a grown
man should be thinking of his mother?

CARMEN

Of course not. I admire a man who thinks of his
mother.

JOSÉ

She doesn't know about all the changes in my life.
I know that what she wants is for me to settle down
with some nice girl. I know she wants grandchildren.
I think she's lonely.

CARMEN

We could go see her. Maybe spend some time with her.

JOSÉ

No, I wouldn't want to spoil the vision of me she has.
She wants me to show up at her doorstep with a plain

little girl wearing flat shoes and carrying a book. You
know how old women are—everything has to line up
just right to spell out the word *familia* or they just don't
get it.

CARMEN

She wouldn't like me?

JOSÉ

She'd get used to you after a while.

CARMEN

Get used to me? You get used to dandruff, not people!

JOSÉ

Anyway, I have plans for us. You help these guys pull
this caper off, and we can get out of here. Maybe find a
place in San Juan. Near the beach. One of those gated
communities they advertise for vacations. It would be
like a whole new life for you. Clean. Fresh air. Safe.

CARMEN

I don't want to move to San Juan. I don't have any
family there.

JOSÉ

If you're with me, then you'll live where I say.

CARMEN

Am I with you now, José? If your mother walked down the street right now, would I be with you?

JOSÉ

What are you talking about? Look, I'm telling you the way it is. Don't get in my face. I don't like it! You and me, we belong together—like you said before . . . something about feeling pain. I liked that. We've got pain holding us together.

CARMEN

Pain? Not love? José, maybe we need to slow this train down. I don't know if I'm ready to make a lifetime thing of this.

JOSÉ

Carmen, don't. . . . Don't think of being away from me. I've given up my whole career on the force for you. It's going to be me and you. Don't even *think* about it being any other way. You don't want me disappointed in you. That would really piss me off.

CARMEN

Don't piss you off? Tell me, Don José, O brave one who gets pissed off: When you were a boy, did you hide behind your mother's legs when the big boys came after you?

JOSÉ

Do yourself a favor, Carmen. Take my mother's name
from your lips.

CARMEN

(edging close to JOSÉ)

What will you put on my lips to replace her name?

She is leaning against him, but he pushes her away.

JOSÉ

You don't understand. You will never understand what
is between me and my mother.

CARMEN

I don't understand, and I don't *want* to understand! I
thought you loved me.

JOSÉ

I love you in a different way, Carmen. You're like . . .

CARMEN

A flower? A rose? Something that you can own? I don't
think so, baby.

JOSÉ

(embarrassed as people are looking at him)

Carmen, sit down. We don't need to put our business
in the street.

OLD MAN IN THE CORNER
It's okay, I don't mind. There's nothing on television, anyway.

CARMEN
(*clearly hurt*)
José, I don't know what you need. I know it's not me.

JOSÉ
Carmen, baby, you don't understand. It's like you're a part of me. When you become a part of someone, it's forever. So when you talk about José, you're talking about Carmen, too. We belong to each other and with each other!

CARMEN
I don't belong to anyone!

JOSÉ
Don't push me.

For a moment, the two stand toe to toe, then CARMEN turns and walks over to where MERCEDES and FRASQUITA are sitting on one side of the stage. JOSÉ goes to sit on the other side.

RAIMONDO
(*trying to break the tension*)
I have to go make a delivery. You, pretty boy, keep an eye on the door. Don't let any crooked cops in here. Ha!

RAIMONDO exits.

TERESA, an older woman, enters. She is very dark-skinned and wears a blue bandana around her head from which wisps of gray hair protrude. Her eyes are large, and her fingernails are painted dark green. She is wearing large gold earrings.

FRASQUITA
(trying to settle CARMEN down)
Carmen, forget him. Look—Teresa is here. Let's have her tell our fortunes.

MERCEDES
I'm due to hit the lottery, but I don't want to play unless today's the day.

CARMEN
(glances at JOSÉ and then away)
Why not? She can tell us how wonderful we're going to be living soon.

The three girls shepherd TERESA to a table.

TERESA
(in a wonderfully husky voice)
I'm thirsty.

FRASQUITA
What do you want?

TERESA

Cappuccino.

MERCEDES signals to a man behind the bar, who starts making the cappuccino.

TERESA opens her purse and takes out a pack of cards, which she shuffles and lays out facedown.

MERCEDES
(lightly)
The cards don't lie.

FRASQUITA
They'll tell us what the future holds.

CARMEN
They'll speak our destinies.

TERESA places her hands over the cards, closes her eyes, nods, and then turns the first one over.

TERESA
You will meet a young man. He has a job in an office.

MERCEDES
Young. But old enough to drive?

TERESA

Old enough to drive, and he leads many men.

MERCEDES

He's in the army. How much does a general make?

TERESA

Everybody looks up to him!

MERCEDES

Oh, my God, it's that cute quarterback that won the
Super Bowl!

TERESA

He loves you very much. He adores you!

MERCEDES

Do you have a name? Does he have a tattoo?

TERESA

You are lucky. The cards have spoken well of your
future.

FRASQUITA

Do me!

*TERESA gathers the cards and once again shuffles them and lays them
out facedown. She then begins to turn them over.*

TERESA

Hah! You will marry an old man. He has been married before, but still he wants you.

FRASQUITA

Mine's old! Pooh. How old? But look, diamonds! He's going to be rich. Old and rich. Not good, but I'll take it.

MERCEDES

Look how much mine loves me! I'd better start taking vitamins.

FRASQUITA

Will we have a big house?

TERESA

In the Bronx.

FRASQUITA

An old man in a big house in the Bronx? That's no fun.

TERESA

More bad news: he dies.

FRASQUITA

Oh, look—he's going to die. Poor thing. But wait—he leaves me all his money. I'll be a rich widow! Yes! Yes! I'll wear my black toreador pants to the funeral, the ones with the sequins.

TERESA

He dies, but such things happen. We cannot put our
hands up against the winds of fate.

CARMEN

Teresa, do my fortune.

*TERESA looks up at CARMEN. She brings her hand to her forehead and
closes her eyes for a moment. She exhales heavily.*

TERESA

I am too tired.

CARMEN

No, Teresa. I need you to do mine.

*TERESA hands the cards to CARMEN, who kisses them up to heaven
and then hands them back. TERESA shuffles them, lays them out, and
begins to turn them over.*

CARMEN

Oh, no! Diamonds, then spades—death! I see it
clearly. First him and then me. Here, give me the cards.

*CARMEN gathers up the cards and takes the rest of the deck from
TERESA as MERCEDES and FRASQUITA go off to one side, still
talking about their good luck. CARMEN frantically shuffles the cards
herself, then lays them out and begins to turn them over.*

CARMEN

Again! Two deaths! Two destinies intertwined. The cards come up one by one to speak of my doom. Let me shuffle them again.

(*She does so.*)

Again and again I shuffle them, turn them up, but it's always the same....

CARMEN throws the cards down and staggers to a table.

CARMEN

Teresa, what's wrong with these cards?

TERESA

They're only cards, Carmen. They don't know how to lie.

FRASQUITA and MERCEDES go to CARMEN.

FRASQUITA

Carmen, come with us. We'll go case out the company. It'll be fun.

CARMEN

One minute.

CARMEN shuffles the cards again. Again she lays them out and turns them over one by one.

CARMEN

Muerte, siempre muerte.

FRASQUITA

(at the door)

Carmen?

CARMEN looks away for a moment, then forces a smile and follows her friends out.

JOSÉ has been sitting in the corner, facing away from the stage. TERESA walks over to him and touches his shoulder. JOSÉ brushes her hand roughly away and turns again toward the wall, lost in his own thoughts.

MICAELA enters from a side door. She looks around nervously and is clearly upset by the sinister look of the room. She spots JOSÉ in a corner, takes a tentative step toward him, then stops. She crosses herself and begins to pray aloud.

MICAELA

I pray that one day he will see me. I pray, O Lord, I have
so much to give but nothing that pleases him. I have
this heart he doesn't want, these arms so ready for him.
I'm so in need, and all he wants is her! O God, please
give me this moment. Let him see me at last, O Lord.

MICAELA hears a commotion from the front of the club and steps into a darkened corner.

JOSÉ stands quickly and points his gun at the door as ESCAMILLO enters.

ESCAMILLO
Relax, cowboy! It's only me. Drinks for everybody!

JOSÉ
They don't serve drinks here. This is a social club. Only coffee and sodas. They don't want the police raiding them on some phony liquor charge.

ESCAMILLO
Good thinking. You have to be focused. Give me an iced tea.
            (*gesturing to the gun*)
You need to be careful with that thing.

JOSÉ
I don't expect a big name like Escamillo to come rushing in here every day.

ESCAMILLO
You're right. Usually, I'm in my corporate offices, taking care of serious business. If I pull off this concert this weekend—and I will—it'll be the start of the greatest tour you've seen. Bigger than Lil Wayne, Shakira, and Beyoncé combined.

JOSÉ
So what are you doing here?

ESCAMILLO

I'm looking for a certain girl. I've only met her once,
but somehow she stays in my head.

JOSÉ

With all the girls following you around the world, you
actually remember one of them? She must be beautiful.

ESCAMILLO

Beautiful, but not available. That's what I've been
told. They say she leaves men lying in her wake the
way a ship leaves dead fish in the water, gasping and
confused.

JOSÉ

So why would you be interested in her?

ESCAMILLO

I don't know. Maybe because I've always wanted what
other men have said is not available. When I lived in
the projects, I wanted to be rich. I used to look up into
the sky and envy people flying high above me. Now
when I look down from my private jet, I wonder if
there's some small boy looking up in envy of me as I
soar overhead.

JOSÉ

Do you have her address?

ESCAMILLO

No, but I'll give a reward to the one who leads me to her. She's beautiful, as you said, and she used to be in love with a cop.

JOSÉ

A police officer?

ESCAMILLO

I say *cop*; you say *police officer*. Interesting. Yes, some poor fool who thought he could hold her because he's had some experience with crackheads.

JOSÉ

I think you'd better watch your mouth, *maricón*.

ESCAMILLO

¿*Maricón?* Ah, I get it. You have a personal interest in this adventure, eh?

JOSÉ

Do I? Tell me, what's this girl called?

ESCAMILLO

Carmen. Let me say the name slowly for you so you can enjoy the sound of it coming from my mouth. *Caaarmen.* Or shall I say, "Officer, her name is Carmen."

JOSÉ

Yes, you're right. I am the policeman she loves.

ESCAMILLO

Loved. Past tense. Once upon a time in a galaxy far
away!

The two men cross the stage toward each other.

JOSÉ

As a policeman, I've handled plenty of fools like you.

ESCAMILLO

Don't let the thousand-dollar suit fool you, Tex, or
whatever your name is. Under these fancy threads is
a ghetto heart direct from the projects, and you have
never dealt with someone like me before.

*JOSÉ rushes across the stage and attempts to hit ESCAMILLO with his
gun butt. ESCAMILLO sidesteps the blow and hits JOSÉ in the small
of his back. The two men start tussling. Soon ESCAMILLO is on the
ground. JOSÉ aims his gun at ESCAMILLO.*

*DANCAIRO, RAIMONDO, and CARMEN enter. CARMEN kneels over
ESCAMILLO, shielding him from JOSÉ.*

RAIMONDO

What's going on?

DANCAIRO
They must be fighting over Carmen.

RAIMONDO
Look, we don't want any fighting in here. We don't need any weight on this place. We've got a good thing going, and we can't mess it up because you guys are chasing the same skirt.

DANCAIRO
Have a drink. Relax.

RAIMONDO
Relax.

CARMEN, suddenly confident again, strides, with hands on hips, to center stage.

CARMEN
Men have to fight. It's their nature. But Raimondo is trying to run a business here. You understand that, don't you, Escamillo?

ESCAMILLO
Yes, yes, of course. But I'm glad it was you, Carmen, who saved me from this madman. I owe you.

JOSÉ
We have unsettled business!

ESCAMILLO

I'll find a way to accommodate you, my friend. You
won't be hard to find. I have a dog trained to sniff out
gutter rats.

DANCAIRO barely restrains JOSÉ, who lunges forward.

ESCAMILLO

But before I go, I want to invite you all to my big
concert this weekend. Madison Square Garden. Just
tell the ticket men that you are from
(*looks around*)
Lillas's place. And a special invitation to you, Carmen.

He kisses her hand, then exits.

RAIMONDO
(*relieved*)

Everybody take it easy! Somebody go down to the
pizza shop and bring back some pies. Put on some
music. I need some noise up in here! Some noise!

*We hear "El Ritmo del Barrio," 𝄞 the bright, cheerful music heard earlier
in the play. There is a general relaxation, but we also see CARMEN and
JOSÉ looking at each other from across the stage. Slowly CARMEN
starts toward JOSÉ. At first he turns away, but slowly, ever so slowly, he
turns toward her.*

JOSÉ
Carmen! I've ... I've been a fool. ...

He reaches out to her.

MICAELA suddenly runs toward them.

MICAELA
José!

JOSÉ turns and sees MICAELA, but then, love in his eyes, turns back to CARMEN.

JOSÉ
Carmen!

MICAELA
Your mother sent me. She needs to see you!

JOSÉ
What? Oh, tell her that I'll be by this weekend.

MICAELA
She was coughing, and at first
          (glances toward CARMEN)
they thought it was nothing.

JOSÉ
But now ... ?

MICAELA

I've always been brave, José. Throughout my life and no matter what I've faced. But seeing you here like this ...

JOSÉ

Micaela, don't worry about it. Tell my mother I'll drop by Sunday, maybe Saturday night.

MICAELA

She might not live that long.

JOSÉ

What?

MICAELA

Your mother's dying. She might not make it to the weekend.

JOSÉ
(*to CARMEN*)

I should go.

CARMEN
(*dismissively*)

Yes, yes, of course. You should go.

MICAELA
Please hurry.

JOSÉ
Carmen, I have to go.

CARMEN
I'm not stopping you, José. Go!

JOSÉ
I'll be back, and then we'll settle things!

JOSÉ leaves with MICAELA.

CARMEN stares down DANCAIRO and brushes off a friendly gesture from RAIMONDO. She is about to leave when the radio begins to play ESCAMILLO's theme song, "The Toreador Song." ♪ *CARMEN, by herself and defiantly, dances across the stage. She stops and looks at herself in a mirror.*

CARMEN
Oh, chicky, look at you. Your makeup is ruined. Your mascara runs down your face like black tears. Escamillo wants us to fight against being invisible. I welcome it. I don't want to see this sad face anymore. Oh, chicky, how did you let your heart get broken again?
(*she sings "Love Has Flown Away"*) ♪

Love came to me, but it
Just wasn't for me.
It touched my heart and left it
Lying on the shore, and
Love smiled at me, but it
Just wasn't for me.
It glanced my way with pity, but
I soon knew it had other plans.
Once again my heart was broken;
I was all alone to
Mourn.

Scene 2

*We are outside Madison Square Garden. It is night, and the street is alive
with young fans. A crowd is forming, and OFFICERS SHEA and LANE
are putting barriers in place to hold people back.*

OFFICER SHEA

Escamillo should be paying us overtime for this duty.
You could get crushed in this crowd.

OFFICER LANE

I bet somebody is getting paid big bucks. The
television cameras are being set up over on Seventh
Avenue, and they have their own security.

OFFICER SHEA

I heard he's got two wives. One in New York and one
in the Dominican Republic.

OFFICER LANE

Bad business. Spanish girls will cut your throat when
you're sleeping!

OFFICER SHEA
You think Spanish girls are really all that hot in bed?

OFFICER LANE
I'll settle for one who's awake!

Sergeant ZUNIGA enters.

ZUNIGA
Okay, men, keep your eyes open. Look out for
terrorists.

OFFICER LANE
Yes, sir.

ZUNIGA goes off left.

OFFICER SHEA
Who's he kidding? Terrorists wouldn't attack this
crowd. They only want to kill white people. Look—
here comes Escamillo's entourage now.

*The dimly lit stage grows brighter, and a sign comes down that reads
MADISON SQUARE GARDEN. A parade of "beautiful people" makes
its way to the concert. We hear music in the background, a combination
of hip-hop and Bizet.*

*A small crowd enters, the imposing figure of ESCAMILLO, dressed in all
of his finery, at its center. CARMEN is on his arm. Photographers hover*

all around them. ESCAMILLO is shaking hands and smiling. He stops his entourage (made up of music types and some business types in suits) and whispers into CARMEN's ear. He takes CARMEN's face between his hands and lifts it gently as he kisses her.

ESCAMILLO
I'll be thinking of you while I'm in there. All these suits may have their degrees and old-boy networks, but I have my street smarts—and the most beautiful woman in New York waiting for me. It's almost not fair.

CARMEN
Be careful. I feel danger in the air.

CARMEN and ESCAMILLO kiss again, and then he goes off with his entourage in tow.

CARMEN is standing alone at center stage; we still hear the background music.

MERCEDES and FRASQUITA enter.

MERCEDES
Girl, you are looking good!

CARMEN
Girl, I am *feeling* good.

FRASQUITA

Carmen, he's here!

CARMEN

Who?

MERCEDES

José. I saw him on the avenue. I said hello, and he just
mumbled at me. He doesn't look good at all. He hasn't
shaved, and he's . . . funky!

CARMEN

I told him we were through, that I didn't want to see
him anymore.

FRASQUITA

(*chewing her gum faster*)

What did he say?

CARMEN

He didn't . . . He didn't seem to understand. It was as
if I was just gaming him to pass the time of day. You
ever tell somebody something and they act like you're
speaking another freaking language?

FRASQUITA

Baby, you need to be looking out for that man. José is
not somebody I would turn my back on. Why don't you
come inside with us?

CARMEN

I'll be okay. Right now I don't think I can stand a
crowd. I'm a little jumpy. I need to be alone with
my thoughts for a bit. I told Escamillo I'd meet him
outside so we can make a quick getaway when the
show's over.

MERCEDES

You falling for Escamillo now?

CARMEN

Escamillo and I understand each other. He lives for the
minute, and I'm just one of those minutes. He'll stop
for a while and then move on. No big deal. No forever
after, no *por vida*. I'm back to being Carmen again.

FRASQUITA

Okay, but watch your back, girlfriend. Remember,
José's a cop. You know how sneaky they can be.

CARMEN

Go on, guys. I'll be okay.

FRASQUITA

Carmen, don't forget us when you reach the top, baby.
We don't want anything, but just nod when you see us.
We'll understand.

MERCEDES
And be proud of you!

CARMEN
We'll always be homegirls.

The three girls embrace, and then MERCEDES and FRASQUITA rush off to the concert.

We hear the music of the opening act begin. CARMEN, somewhat uncomfortable in her new role, moves to the beat and leans against a light pole. Then, from out of the shadows, comes JOSÉ. Unshaven, he is wearing a dark hoodie and sneakers. At first he appears drunk, but then we see that he's distorted with rage.

JOSÉ
Carmen!

CARMEN
(shrinking away from him)
José! What . . . ? What are you doing here?

JOSÉ
(his speech slow and hollow)
Carmen, I had to see you. I love you so.

CARMEN
(turning away)
No!

JOSÉ

Love doesn't know such a word as *no*. Love can only know *yes*.

CARMEN

What do you want from my life, José? What do you want? I don't have anything to give you. *¡No más! ¡No más!* I need to be by myself.

JOSÉ
(taking something from his pocket)

Look, I've brought you something. A ring. It's the symbol of my love for you. I give it to you, and my heart goes with it, as your heart came to me with the flower you gave me that sweet day.

CARMEN
(turning away)

I am ruined by love, a bright dayflower lost in his grave, dark eyes.

JOSÉ

Carmen, all I want is your heart. Is that too much to ask?

CARMEN

My heart, a pitiful handful of dust.

JOSÉ gives the ring to CARMEN. She looks at it for a moment, then flings it back at him, hitting him in the chest.

JOSÉ

No! Your heart is everything to me, Carmen, everything! You said you loved me.

CARMEN

Take it back, José. I don't want it, or you. You have no love to give. You just have your darkness. I'm afraid of you.

JOSÉ

Carmen! That was my mother's ring, and I gave it to you. You need me. I'm all you have in this world!

CARMEN

I gave you my heart once, José. But what we had was never real love. You planted a lie in my heart, and I nourished it too eagerly. We're through.

JOSÉ

Give me one more chance.

CARMEN

Never! Never!

JOSÉ

So that you can laugh at me in Escamillo's arms?

So that the two of you can think of me and smile? You can't do this to me! You can't *do this to me!*

CARMEN tries to run, but José quickly catches her. She desperately tries to push away from him, and he just as desperately clings to her. ESCAMILLO's theme, "The Toreador Song" 𝄞, begins to play from inside the Garden.

CARMEN
José, please leave me alone. Let me lead my life in peace. You have somebody—that girl. Go with her and leave me in peace.

JOSÉ falls to his knees and puts his arms around CARMEN's legs.

JOSÉ
Carmen, you can't leave me. You need me. Admit it! From the first time you saw me, you needed me. You need me!

ESCAMILLO's theme rises as CARMEN and JOSÉ struggle in the semi-darkness. In the background, the crowd noises become louder, as does the music.

JOSÉ
Where are you going? To be with him? To be with him while the world looks at me like some kind of freak to be pitied? Never, Carmen. Never, do you hear me? You need me. You will always need me!

JOSÉ pulls a gun from under his coat.

CARMEN

Fate closes the day.

JOSÉ

Carmen, I love you so much. You have to believe me.

CARMEN

Stars all look away.

JOSÉ

There is nothing in life but the two of us! Nothing!

CARMEN

Death opens her arms. She says, "Come to me."

JOSÉ

I won't give you to Escamillo.

CARMEN

(sings the "Destiny Theme") 🎼

Life laughs at me now,
Sad, forsaken clown.
Dreams crumble and fall.
They die silently.

JOSÉ

We will always be together.

CARMEN

Where is there to turn to?
Where can I find mercy?
Love is what I needed,
All I wanted from this life.

CARMEN pushes away from JOSÉ one last time and desperately looks for a way into Madison Square Garden. JOSÉ aims his gun and shoots. CARMEN gasps, clutches her side, and falls.

JOSÉ

Carmen, I love you! I love you!

The two figures are silhouetted on the stage. JOSÉ leans over CARMEN's prone body as the music continues in the background.

Slowly, the stage grows dark, and we continue to hear the melancholy sound of the ominous theme we have heard several times before.

Then, in the darkness, we once again hear "El Ritmo del Barrio" 𝄞, the cheerful, lively music we heard toward the beginning of the play.

The End

Author's Note

WHY ANOTHER *CARMEN*?

I first heard excerpts from the opera *Carmen*, by Georges Bizet, as a ten-year-old in a music appreciation class in Harlem. The music was brilliant and the story, as our teacher described it, exciting. Some of the music even sounded vaguely familiar.

Harlem was full of music when I was growing up. If you started on 125th Street at Broadway and made your way cross town toward the East River, you could actually hear the music change as you walked by different blocks. Broadway was Irish and German, and that was the music coming from the small bakeries and butcher shop we frequented.

At St. Nicholas Avenue the neighborhood turned into a mixture of races, and the music in the record shops along the most famous Harlem thoroughfare was African American. The blues blared out from speakers hanging by wires outside of shops so narrow you had to turn sideways to get into them. Harlem above 125th Street had become the Black cultural center of America. Churches shared the streets with nightclubs, funeral parlors, and shady jazz clubs. Across from Blumstein's, the department store, a small shop sold gospel records.

As you neared the Apollo Theater it was all jazz. As a kid I listened to live bands led by Duke Ellington, Count Basie, and Cab Calloway. This was the music that Harlem became known for and, unlike today's music, which is heard mostly on individual iPods, it filled the streets.

The next change along Harlem's main drag came as you passed

Lenox Avenue on the East Side. Suddenly there was a Latino beat in the air, a beat that sometimes mixed with Harlem jazz and sometimes stood alone. Latino musicians had been around for years in Harlem, playing mostly in smaller clubs, at house parties, and at picnics in the local parks. East Harlem had once been primarily Italian, but by the end of the First World War (1919) the population had changed dramatically. Puerto Ricans, Cubans, Dominicans, Mexicans, and Brazilians lived and worked in these streets, and they brought their music with them. The famous Harlem Hellfighters Jazz Band had more than a dozen musicians from Puerto Rico alone. Latino music became very popular, and by the time the classically trained composer and percussionist Tito Puente came along in the late forties, both Harlem and the outside world were ready for him.

This mixing of peoples in Harlem strongly influenced the rest of New York's culture as well. Spanish poets such as Juan Ramón Jiménez and Federico García Lorca were attracted to the vibrant life in East Harlem, heard its music, and were affected by this thriving community. But cultural exchanges are not new—the opera *Carmen* itself reflects its French composer's ideas of Spanish culture.

Georges Bizet himself borrowed the story from another Frenchman, Prosper Mérimée (1803–1870), a novelist and historian who wrote *Carmen* as a novella.

I liked *Carmen* when I first heard it as a ten-year-old, despite the fact that I didn't know where Spain was, had never seen a bullfight, and didn't know the opera's history. When I grew older I learned that there was more than one version of *Carmen*. That was a bit of a shock because I thought you couldn't mess with "classical" music.

The first version of *Carmen* that I actually saw was *Carmen Jones*, starring Dorothy Dandridge and Harry Belafonte. This all-black movie was based on a musical, also all black, first performed on Broadway in 1943. The movie came out in 1954, the year I dropped out of high school, and I saw it at an Army base in New Jersey. While the music was still intriguing, I thought the story line was trite. Carmen, played by the lovely Dorothy Dandridge, worked in a parachute factory instead of a cigarette factory, and Don José was a soldier. But what bothered me most about the film was that the lyrics of the songs were changed to black stereotypes. The "Gypsy Song," beautiful in the original opera, was now reduced to "Beat Out Dat Rhythm on a Drum." "La Habanera" became "Dat's Love." In short, I felt that the lyricist, Oscar Hammerstein II, was looking down on black people.

The French of Mérimée's time would have considered the poor people of Carmen's class exotic. Parts of Spain, the setting of Mérimée's novella, had been ruled by the Moors, people from North Africa, until the fifteenth century. The term *Moors* is used in many ways and is not precise but, generally, it refers to people who have some North African heritage. When, in the novella, Mérimée says that he thinks that Carmen's copper-colored skin and coarse hair meant that she was a Moor, he was accurately describing many of the people I have seen in that part of Spain.

In Mérimée's time the city of Seville, in Spain, was the cigarette capital of the world. Thousands of young women worked in the industry rolling cigarettes by hand. These were not good-paying jobs, and the women who worked in the factories were often looked down upon. Neither Mérimée's novella nor Bizet's opera give much background for Carmen herself. It was enough for them to think of her as simply "different."

There have been many versions of *Carmen*, from a silent screen version to countless stage versions. Some productions treat Carmen as an independent woman who could have an affair or openly flirt with soldiers because her norms were different than those of white European women. But as I approached this project, I knew I wanted to treat this fascinating young woman with the respect she deserves.

Many opera and film directors have moved the time, setting, and medium of their productions to update the work and make it speak to their own era. Some have moved the time from the mid-nineteenth century to the later nineteenth century and even the twentieth century. In recent years there have been stunning dance versions, for me the absolute best being a breathtaking flamenco performance—captured on film—directed by Carlos Saura. Matthew Bourne's version, called *The Car Man*, depicted a gay dance performance. Joseph Gaï Ramaka's film, *Karmen Geï*, takes place in Senegal, West Africa.

However *Carmen* is performed, each version works because of the strength of its characters, as well as the strength of its music. Bizet's own music tells the story brilliantly. In *Carmen: A Hip Hopera*, starring Beyoncé, the music never rises above the ordinary, and the production becomes just another run-of-the-mill urban flick.

For a while I lost interest in *Carmen*, primarily because opera performances are simply too expensive in this country. To me the point of opera is the whole stage presentation along with the music. I didn't just want to hear the music. If you couldn't afford to go see a stage production, why bother?

But when I read the original novella by Mérimée again, I found a lot more in the story than most stagings display. In the original story the character of Don José is much more sinister. He's really a nut job that Carmen happens upon. Carmen herself is a shady character who accepts a life of crime as her lot in life, but I saw her independence not as an example of some kind of women's liberation but as a needed strength in a very hard world, a world I thought I knew.

I see Carmen as a young, tough Dominican woman who has done the best she can in an environment that is ready to use her and abuse her if she allows it. But she is also tired of this life and sees, in José, a love interest that might be her way out. Having lived most of my life in this same kind of setting, I knew I was feeling Carmen in a big way.

The idea rested in the back of my head for years until, one day after watching yet another light version of the opera, I happened into my local bodega to buy milk. There was an animated conversation among the three cashiers—mostly in Spanish, with a smattering of English—and a lot of finger pointing toward the door where someone who had offended them had just gone through. I was reminded of the fight scene between the factory girls at the beginning of the opera. And they were much closer in my mind to the real factory girls from Seville than the carefully gowned women in the opera I had seen. Also, they were all very young, as I thought the girls should have been. But where was my Carmen?

Then the door opened and my Carmen walked in! She was beautiful, young, and pissed! Some dude had done her wrong, and she proceeded to tell the other girls. I wanted to rush right home and start writing.

When approaching my own version I gave myself several rules. The first was to respect my characters! Carmen would not be flirtatious simply because she was Latina or just to satisfy the story line. She needed to have fully rounded human desires. The second was to respect the community in which the story takes place.

The music to *Carmen* is readily available through the Internet. Recorded versions can be rented and the original score is out of copyright, so school and small theater performances are quite possible. I still love Bizet's original music, but I didn't think much of the lyrics; I felt the words needed to be changed to fit a modern setting. One set of lyrics I really didn't like was "The Toreador Song." As a young writer I was commissioned to do a magazine piece on bullfighting and had attended my first one in Lima, Peru. It wasn't at all to my taste and I haven't seen a bullfight since. I think of Escamillo more as a businessman with the bravado of a bullfighter who has his hand in a number of fields. But it is Escamillo who raps over the background and who represents, to Carmen, yet another opportunity to move out of the cycle of despair that is so much a part of inner-city life.

The ending of *Carmen* is tragic, and the music Bizet created for it, which I have called the "Destiny Theme," portends the fatal drama. I was so moved by this music that, as I wrote, it was constantly on my mind. But it was one of the pieces written by Bizet to separate the acts of the opera, called Entr'actes, that I felt expressed Carmen's character even more. This piece, often played as a flute solo with a harp or guitar background, is beautiful and hopeful—as I saw Carmen—and yet there is a haunting melancholy to it as well.

This piece reflects how I see Carmen, a young Latina woman searching for love but finding, instead, yet another man willing to sacrifice her for his own very dark reasons. I asked my friend, Kwame Brandt-Pierce, an arranger and composer, to add a Latino beat to this piece. Over a snack of sangria, Italian bread, and black olives, my editor and I worked with the young composer/arranger to decide how we would handle this portion of the music. His arrangements of Bizet are spectacular and stirring and will undoubtedly become part of the legend that is Carmen. You can download them at www.egmontusa.com or www.walterdeanmyers.net.

Stories work because they touch the hearts of the audience they are trying to reach. I hope this version of *Carmen* touches your heart.

About the Music

The story of *Carmen*—as are the stories of all operas—is told in many ways, each having its own purpose, meaning, and flair. A composer learns of, or imagines a story that he or she would like to tell. Perhaps he found a novella or play that inspired him, or she came across a historical event that intrigued her? Or perhaps even a melody suggested a story?

Once an opera is started, there are many elements for its creators to consider. There is a libretto, which is the writing out of the story, complete with dialogue. The dialogue might be spoken or, in most operas, sung.

Carmen began as a short novel and was later performed as a play. Something in the story attracted the young composer Georges Bizet (1838–1875) and he began working on the piece, completing it in 1874.

The libretto, the text of an opera, tells the story in a straightforward manner. The composer understands that the play will be acted, and he must rely on the writer to give the opera sufficient action to make the viewing interesting. So the libretto tells the story, but that is not the only way the story is told. It is also conveyed through the actors and by their costumes and the set design.

Sometimes there is dancing in an opera, and the dancers contribute to the movement and entertainment of the work, but they also aid in the laying out of the story.

However, it is the music, the score, that is the chief medium of an opera. The score must reflect the emotions being portrayed onstage, and at this, Bizet, in *Carmen*, absolutely rocked!

Another way of learning the story of an opera, which is often overlooked, is in the programs handed out to a theater audience. If you don't know the story of an opera, and you can't understand the words, how will you know what's going on? Some opera performances today have subtitles on a monitor, but if you don't know the plot before you take your seat, it's difficult to appreciate the full range of the opera you're seeing.

When working on this adaptation, I knew that there were things I wanted to say. I wanted to depict Carmen as a tough Latina woman, but one with feelings I've seen in the inner cities across America. Yes, she is tough, but she is also very, very human. She needs love and affection as we all do. I looked at what Bizet was doing with the music and the story, and I knew I could translate it to this year, this time.

Although the original French lyrics created by Henri Meilhac and Ludovic Halévy are dated, the music still works. If a different setting is used, then the words are sometimes changed to fit that setting. I chose a modern urban setting to write *Carmen* but always with the original in mind.

Songs

All music composed by Georges Bizet

---

1. El Ritmo del Barrio (variation)
Arranged by Kwame Brandt-Pierce

2. La Habanera

3. La Seguidilla

4. Destiny Theme

5. The Toreador Song

6. Love Has Flown Away

7. Love Has Flown Away (variation)
Arranged by Kwame Brandt-Pierce

"El Ritmo del Barrio" (variation on a theme from *Carmen*)
Arranged by Kwame Brandt-Pierce

Kwame is a young composer-arranger. I asked him to put together some arrangements of Bizet's music that would reflect a modern musical scene. Here he does a spirited and rousing rendition of one of the opera's pieces, an *entr'acte*, by adding merengue rhythm and instrumentation. This version reminded me of the section of Harlem that was called Spanish Harlem, with its mixture of music from the Dominican Republic, Puerto Rico, and Cuba, which is why I use it as the "rhythm of the neighborhood" in this book.

El Ritmo del Barrio

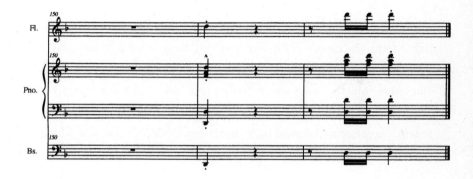

"La Habanera"

Carmen introduces herself through this song. Using a Habanera, a Cuban dance form, she expresses the idea that love, for her, is a risky business. I love this song because I know that love in many inner cities is really risky. But either something she sees in José attracts her, or else she recognizes some need in herself to fall in love. The music is lilting and invites the listener to get up and dance! Bizet understood this Cuban music, which bears a strong African influence.

La Habanera

"La Seguidilla"

Here, Carmen has been arrested for fighting but she challenges José to release her! This is a bold move on her part, and the music for it comes from a Spanish folk dance. The dance involves intricate steps and virtually dares José to respond. Will he give in to her charms? Will he take the risk that this inner-city woman urges and prove his love for her? Or will he turn away and do his duty as a police officer? Carmen tells José to release her and meet her later at a neighborhood club she knows. The women of Bizet's opera, working in a cigarette factory, would have been familiar with this style of music.

La Seguidilla

"Destiny Theme"

Bizet tells us right from the beginning that *Carmen* is going to end badly. Before the story even starts, in the Prelude, we hear the music ending with this dark, foreboding theme. Bad things are going to happen, Bro, and you better get ready for it! The idea of Carmen's death comes up again and again in this opera. Carmen confronts it most directly in the card scene when she sees the prediction of death. But for me, the most ominous sign is this heavy, heavy musical theme.

Destiny Theme

"The Toreador Song"

I don't really believe that Carmen loves Escamillo, this Jay-Z wannabe! What is really going on here is that she sees her relationship with José is seriously wack and that anybody would be better than this dude. But can she break away from him? There is the scene at the concert, and everything seems cool, but Carmen's girlfriends warn her that José is nearby. Escamillo raps over music that is played in the beat of a march. The rhythm here denotes the grand entrance of the toreador (a made-up word—it should be *torero*) into a bullfighting arena, but it could also be a signal that Carmen thinks it is time to move on.

The Toreador Song

"Love Has Flown Away" ("L'Entr'acte," in the original opera)
and
"Love Has Flown Away" (variation on a theme from *Carmen*)
Arranged by Kwame Brandt-Pierce

The term *entr'acte* literally means "between the acts." This music is traditionally played between the acts of an opera or play and can be used to give the actors a breather, allow time to change sets, or to set the mood for what is coming in the next act of the piece. The entr'acte between Acts II and III of *Carmen* is a beautiful piece of music that I love and feel expresses Carmen's realization that, by allowing herself to fall in love again, she's also opened herself up to be hurt again. These are my lyrics, inspired by Bizet's music. Kwame Brandt-Pierce, also inspired by this piece, makes it soar with a pulsating Latin beat suggesting Carmen's return to her roots and away from the troubled José.

Love Has Flown Away

Love Has Flown Away

(variation)

Love Has Flown Away (*variation*).